Over in the Pink House

Over in the Pink House

New Jump Rope Rhymes

by Rebecca Kai Dotlich

Illustrations by Melanie Hall

Wordsong

Boyds Mills Press

For Dana, wherever you are,
and all the jumpers from Falcon Street
—*R. K. D.*

For the illustration gang:
Alice Provensen, Maria Cristina Brusca, James Warhola, and Dirk Zimmer
—*M. H.*

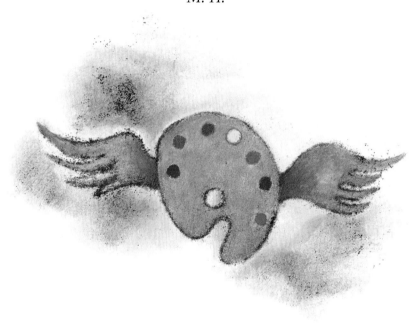

Text copyright © 2004 by Rebecca Kai Dotlich
Illustrations copyright © 2004 by Melanie Hall

Published by Wordsong
Boyds Mills Press, Inc.
A Highlights Company
815 Church Street
Honesdale, Pennsylvania 18431
Printed in China

Publisher Cataloging-in-Publication Data (U.S.)

Dotlich, Rebecca Kai.
    Over in the pink house : new jump rope rhymes / by Rebecca Kai Dotlich ;
illustrations by Melanie Hall.—1st ed.
[32] p. : col. ill. ;   cm.
Summary: Rhymes for young readers to chant during jump rope games.
ISBN 1-59078-027-2
1. Rope skipping — Juvenile literature. 2. Jump rope rhymes — Juvenile literature.
(1. Rope skipping. 2. Jump rope rhymes.) I. Hall, Melanie. II. Title.
796.2 21 GV498.D68 2004
2003108227

First edition, 2004
The text of this book is set in 15-point Minion.

Visit our Web site at www.boydsmillspress.com

10 9 8 7 6 5 4 3 2 1

Contents

Jumping Spell

Candelabra,
blade of grass,
jump inside
a looking glass.
Tap of heel,
holly tree,
he will fall
in love with me.
Jasmine, clove,
jingle bell . . .
will he know it?
Will he tell?
Ink and ivy,
this be true:
He will love me
through and through.

Apple Dumpling

Apple dumpling,
black-eyed pea,
CARVE a heart
into a tree . . .
whose initials
will it show?
Say them six times
in a row:
JW, JW, JW, JW, JW, JW . . .

Over in the Pink House

Over in the pink house,
over in the park,
lives a gang of kittens
meowing in the dark;
one is called Butter,
one is called Lump,
one is called Sugar,
jump,
jump,
jump.

Sea Skip

Tumbling tide and lantern light,
sailors out at sea tonight.
Boats and bridges, nets of fish,
once a captain made a wish:

Moon and trout of rainbow blue,
buckler, fin, and fishtail, too;
toss this letter out to sea. . . .
Will my sweetheart marry me?

Boats and bridges, nets of fish,
once a captain made a wish.
Moon and trout of rainbow blue,
did the captain's wish come true?
Yes, no, yes, no, yes . . .

Cracker and Corn

Soup bean, soup bean,
cracker and corn.
Blackberry muffin,
where were you born?
Born in London?
Born in France?
Born in time for
true romance?
Crossover, crossover,
turn in place . . .
when you STOP,
you'll see his face.

Gingerbread Spin

Spools and spools
of spinners' thread,
spin the brown
of gingerbread;
tie a string
around your thumb,
pluck a berry,
boil a plum.
Spools and spools
of spinners' thread,
spin the brown
of gingerbread . . .
G-I-N-G-E-R-B-R-E-A-D.

Handsome Harry

There goes haughty
Handsome Harry,
met a girl in February;
fell in love in late September,
Handsome Harry can't remember. . . .
There goes Harry,
there goes Harry!
Looking for a girl to marry.

Summer and Snow

Cup of summer,
bowl of snow,
who's the best friend
that you know?
Might be Charlotte,
might be me. . . .
Choose! So everyone can see.

Gold and Copper

Gold and copper candlelight,
stay out jumping late tonight.
Through the gardens,
round the trees,
in the tunnels, on the seas—
skip all the skippers,
hear them call:
Jump in the circle, one and all.
Gold and copper candlelight,
stay out jumping late tonight.

Maybe So

Touch the sidewalk,
touch the sky;
have you ever told a lie?
Could be,
almost,
yes or no . . .
if you miss it—
maybe so.

Rosa, Rosa

Rosa, Rosa,
spin the rope.
Where's the letter
that you wrote. . . .
Kitchen cupboard?
Cellar stair?
In the attic—
no, not *there*.
By the window?
By the light?
In the book
you read last night?
Turn the page,
turn the page,
there it is!

Honey on Hot Cakes

Honey on hot cakes,
jam on toast,
it's my turn to
jump the most . . .
ten is good,
twenty is best;
turn around,
turn around
to the west.
Honey on hot cakes,
jam on toast,
it's my turn to jump
the *most*.

Pizza, Pizza

Pepperoni.
Cheese on top.
Spin the rope
around and *stop*.
Add an onion
to the pie;
add another,
time to cry.
Hottest peppers
from a jar—
spin it *faster*,
you'll go far.

love to the Family

EETINGS from Madrid

Postcard Jump

Tin of tea, bag of beans,
postcard from the Philippines.
Candy apple, cherry tree,
how many postcards will there be?
One from Finland,
two from Spain,
three delivered in the rain.
Four from Turkey,
then one more . . .
number five's from Singapore.
Pick a postcard.
Pick one, pick—
read it, read it, read it
quick!

Jump Rope Jack and Jellyfish

Seashell, wind spell,
ruby ring;
sack of crystals
tied with string.
Jump Rope Jack
     and Jellyfish,
jump three times and
make a wish . . .
peacock feather, sea glass, too;
may this one wish come to you.
Jump again, *jump* again,
it came true.

Lily, Lily

Lily, Lily, dressed in white.
Will you win the prize tonight?
Will your jump be 102,
all the way to Timbuktu?
Lily, Lily, don't be last—
twirl it,
twirl it,
twirl it fast . . .
four more,
three more,
two more,
one!
Lily, Lily, you have *won*.

Jungle Jump

Tiger, tiger, cat's meow.
Jump on in and show us how.
Lion, lion, give a roar,
dance on through the jungle door;
snakes of poison by your feet—
hot potato, hotter street.
Faster, faster, whoosh and swing,
tiger, tiger, hear it sing . . .
monkey, zebra, hippo snout,
there's the door—
you're out, you're out!

Alligator Stomp

Hurry, Harry, get the waiter.
Sir, we ordered alligator!
Waiter, waiter, we can't wait,
bring him on a fancy plate.
Wait a minute! What's this stuff?
Alligator meat is tough.
Take him back and make us smile—
bring a plate of crocodile.

Pancake Song

Hilda, Hilda, mix the batter.
Pour the pancakes. What's the matter?
Pour them perfect if you can—
silver dollars in the pan.
Sizzle, sizzle, flip them high.
Turn around and say good-bye.

Hannah, Hannah

Hannah, Hannah,
from Savannah,
ate a solid green banana.
Hear her belly start to moan?
Better let her
jump back home.

Love in Rhyme

Lavender lilac,
baby blue,
will he love me
through and through?

Cherry blossom,
tiny stem,
if he does,
will I love him?

Is it yes?
Is it no?
Trip just once
and *out* you go!

Royal Round

Hop on one foot, hop on two.
King's address is Waterloo;
through the windows,
hear him snore
all the way to Salvador.

Here's the castle, jump on in.
Jump three times around,
then spin.
Old King's crown is yours to keep;
who is quickest on her feet?

Robe of velvet, jeweled crown.
You'll be carried through the town;
jump three times, then turn about.
Leave the castle!
Jump on out!

Jillian Jump

Jillian, Jillian,
where will you go?
   To Denmark,
   To Sweden,
   to pick out a beau.
Jillian, Jillian,
what will you wear?
   A jewel on my hat
   and a rose in my hair.
Jillian, Jillian,
who will you find?
   A prince of a prince;
   a one of a kind.
Jillian, Jillian,
what will you say?
   I'd like a glass shoe
   and a peony bouquet.
Jillian, Jillian,
if he says no?
   I'll be on my way
   to find a new beau.

Cookies

Cookie cutter,
cookie tin—
Mama's cookies!
Jump right in.
Raisin,
sugar,
chocolate chip,
peanut butter,
lick your lip . . .
one,
two,
three,
four,
butterscotch,
and that's one more.

Penny and Pudding

Penny, Penny,
loaf of bread.
Buy a bonnet
for your head.
Pudding, pudding,
pocket dough.
Where did all the
money go?
Three coins,
two coins,
one coin,
gone.

If It's Monday

If it's Monday, kiss your sister.
If it's Tuesday, meet a mister.
If it's Wednesday, call the nurse.
If it's Thursday, buy a purse.
If it's Friday, give a shake.
If it's Saturday, bake a cake.
If it's Sunday, ring a bell. . . .
Clap your hands and shout farewell!

Kettle and Can

Teapot, teapot,
kettle and can.
Mixer, masher,
pudding and pan.
One to pour,
two to mix.
Three to boil,
four to fix.
Cook's in the kitchen—
cook's in the hall—
now there's no one,
now there's no one,
now there's no one
left
at
all.

Catch the Coin

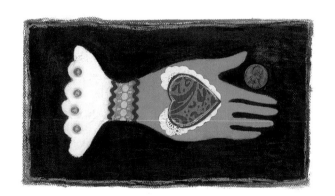

Catch a penny.
Catch a dime.
Will he be my Valentine?
Throw another,
one more still—
catch the coin and *yes*,
he will.

Down in the Dungeon

Down in the dungeon,
dark and deep;
silent skippers
fast asleep.
Carry candles
down the stair . . .
who will still be
sleeping there?
One, two, three, four,
wake up, skippers—
out the door!

Cottage Cradle

Cottage cradle.
August sky.
Teapot, teardrop,
lullaby.
Rose and ramble.
Shell and stone.
Gumdrop, lollipop.
Ice-cream cone.
Sing to the baby,
sing to the baby,
sing to the baby,
all
night
long.

Plum Puddle Town

Sophie in a silver gown
skips around Plum Puddle town,
naming squares of cobblestone—
castor bean and knucklebone,
soursop and paper flower,
carriage key and April shower.
Sophie in a silver gown
skips around Plum Puddle town,
naming squares of cobblestone—
hollyhock and herringbone . . .
Sophie in a silver gown,
Sophie in Plum Puddle town.

HOLLYHOCK, CASTOR BEAN, KNUCKLEBONE, SOURSOP, P

APRIL SHOWER

Biddle Beddle

Bustle, bustle,
biddle, beddle,
do you know a girl named Gretel?
Yes, oh yes, I know her well,
and I know her sister Belle.
Gretel lives on Tuppence Lane;
Belle lives by the sea in Maine.
I know *them* and they know me.
Bustle, bustle,
biddle bee.